Thomas' New Friend

Based on
The Railway Series

by the

Rev. W ....

Illus........

Rob.... ....

EGMONT

EGMONT

We bring stories to life

First published in Great Britain in 2017
by Egmont UK Limited
The Yellow Building, 1 Nicholas Road, London W11 4AN

Thomas the Tank Engine & Friends™

CREATED BY BRITT ALLCROFT

Based on the Railway Series by the Reverend W Awdry
© 2017 Gullane (Thomas) LLC. Thomas the Tank Engine & Friends and
Thomas & Friends are trademarks of Gullane (Thomas) Limited.
Thomas the Tank Engine & Friends and Design is Reg. U.S. Pat. & Tm. Off.
© 2017 HIT Entertainment Limited.

HiT entertainment

ISBN 978 1 4052 8584 1
66572/1
Printed in Italy

Stay safe online. Egmont is not responsible for content hosted by third parties.

Written by Emily Stead. Designed by Claire Yeo.
Series designed by Martin Aggett.

FSC
MIX
Paper
FSC® C018306

Egmont is passionate about helping to preserve the world's remaining ancient forests.
We only use paper from legal and sustainable forest sources.

This book is made from paper certified by the Forest Stewardship Council® (FSC®),
an organisation dedicated to promoting responsible management of forest resources.
For more information on the FSC, please visit www.fsc.org. To learn more about Egmont's
sustainable paper policy, please visit www.egmont.co.uk/ethical

*When I caused an accident
at the Docks, I thought I'd be in
trouble. I made up an engine called
Geoffrey to take the blame,
but everyone wanted to
meet my new friend!*

One day on Sodor, Thomas was in a hurry. He wasn't looking where he was going, and bashed into a line of trucks. **Bash!**

Cranky was lowering a crate, but the trucks had shunted Cranky's flatbed up the track.

The crate **smashed** open on the rails, and out **jumped** hundreds of bouncy balls! Some **splashed** into the sea!

"Somebody **shoved** us!" moaned a truck.

Thomas backed away, feeling bad. "It wasn't me," he pretended. "It was, er, Geoffrey!"

"Geoffrey?" called Cranky. "I can't see any other engines around here."

Everyone wanted to hear about Geoffrey, but there **was** no Geoffrey. Thomas had made him up! Next, Thomas was passing the Steamworks.

"Hello, Thomas," said Victor. "Tell me about Geoffrey. Is he a Steamie?"

"Er, that's right," Thomas mumbled. "He's a big red Steamie from the Mainland."

And Thomas puffed quickly away.

Soon, everyone was talking about Geoffrey.

"I don't suppose he's very **fast**," huffed Gordon.

"He is," said Percy. "He's so **fast** that no one even saw him leave the Docks!"

"A strange engine on my Railway?" The Fat Controller said. "Please take me to him, Thomas."

"But Geoffrey is very shy, Sir," Thomas puffed.

The Fat Controller insisted. Thomas had to think quickly.

"I can't take you, Sir," he said. "Geoffrey is, er, hiding . . . in Henry's Tunnel!"

"Well, I'm sure we'll find him," said The Fat Controller, scratching his head.

"I'll warn Geoffrey you're coming," Thomas called. And he steamed away – **backwards** – before anyone could tell him to stop!

Thomas sped along, with Percy and The Fat Controller chasing after. Percy's wheels felt funny, rolling backwards at such speed.

"Wait, Thomas!" Percy **peeped**. "What's wrong?"

Annie and Clarabel told Thomas to slow down, but Thomas pumped his pistons even faster.

When Percy arrived at Henry's Tunnel,
Thomas was nowhere to be seen.

"He must be inside, Sir," Percy said.

The Fat Controller climbed down from the cab.
"Thomas? Geoffrey? Are you in there?" he called.

"Yes, Sir," Thomas replied.

"Will you come out, please, Geoffrey?"
The Fat Controller said.

Thomas pretended to be Geoffrey. "I can't, Sir.
I'm too shy," he called, in a funny voice.

"Shy or not, you have caused confusion and
delay," **boomed** The Fat Controller.

"I'm sorry, Sir," said Thomas, still pretending
to be Geoffrey. "I'll be good from now on."

Thomas' plan had worked! Everyone thought Geoffrey was real! Then there was trouble . . . The rails began to **rumble** . . . Spencer was racing up behind Thomas at full speed!

"Fizzling fireboxes!" Thomas wheeshed, steaming out of the tunnel.

Sparks flew from Spencer's brakes. **Screech!** He stopped just in time.

"Where's poor Geoffrey?" said The Fat Controller.

"Who's Geoffrey?" asked Spencer, puzzled.

"He's a red Steamie from the Mainland," Percy explained. "Did you pass him in the tunnel?"

"The only engine I could see was **Thomas**," Spencer huffed.

The Fat Controller was cross.

Thomas knew he had to tell the truth – about the accident and about Geoffrey. "I'm sorry," he said.

"Accidents happen," The Fat Controller replied. "But stories about pretend engines will not do."

"It's a shame Geoffrey isn't real," peeped Percy. "He sounded like a Really Fun Engine!"

Meet The Fat Controller

top hat

black coat

waistcoat

smart shoes

Thomas' challenge to you

Look back through the pages of this book
and see if you can spot:

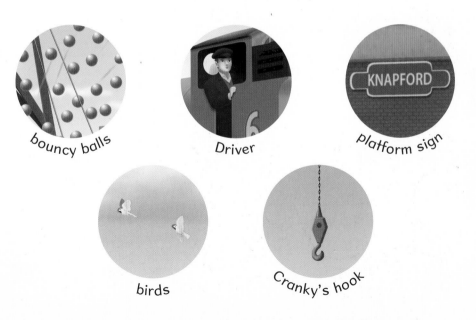

bouncy balls

Driver

platform sign

birds

Cranky's hook

THE *THOMAS* ENGINE ADVENTURES

 Thomas
 Percy
 Harold
 James
 Cranky
 Spencer

 Gordon
 Flynn
 Toby
 Henry
 Hiro
 Emily

 Thomas and Bertie's Race
 Thomas Goes Crash!
 Kevin
 Diesel
 Troublesome Trucks
 Charlie

 The Thomas Way
 Thomas' New Friend
 Oliver
 Victor
 Thomas' Trusty Wheels
 Thomas Helps Hiro

EGMONT